JO'S TRIUMPH

1. Carson City
2. Dayton
3. Miller's
4. Fort Churchill
5. Buckland's
6. Shelly Creek
7. Cold Springs
8. Jacob's Spring
9. Dry Creek
10. Grubb's Well
11. Robert's Creek
12. Sulphur Springs
13. Diamond Springs
14. Jacob's Well
15. Ruby
16. Mountain Springs
17. Cherry Bend
18. Butte
19. Egan Canyon
20. Schell Creek

PONY EXPRESS ROUTE

JO'S TRIUMPH
Nikki Tate

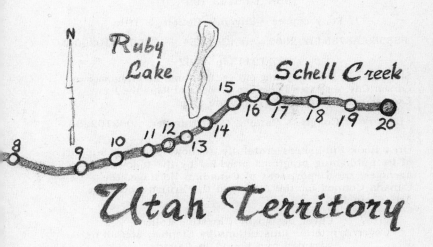

Ruby Lake

Schell Creek

N

8 9 10 11 12 13 14 15 16 17 18 19 20

Utah Territory

ORCA BOOK PUBLISHERS

For Toby in anticipation of future reading adventures and for Dad and Stew, who both urged me to "Go West."

National Library of Canada Cataloguing in Publication Data
Tate, Nikki, 1962-

Jo's triumph

ISBN 1-55143-199-8

1. Pony express--Juvenile fiction. I. Title.

PS8589.A8735J67 2002   jC813'54   C2002-910250-2

PZ7.T2113Jo 2002

Summary: In 1860, a young girl escapes from an orphanage in Carson City, disguises herself as a boy, and joins the Pony Express where danger and adventure await.

Library of Congress Catalog Card Number: 2002102203

Orca Book Publishers gratefully acknowledges the support of its publishing programs provided by the following agencies: the Department of Canadian Heritage, the Canada Council for the Arts, and the British Columbia Arts Council.

Cover design by Christine Toller
Cover & interior illustrations by Stephen McCallum
Printed and bound in Canada

Teachers' guide available.
1-800-210-5277
www.orcabook.com

IN CANADA
Orca Book Publishers
PO Box 5626, Station B
Victoria, BC Canada
V8R 6S4

IN THE UNITED STATES
Orca Book Publishers
PO Box 468
Custer, WA USA
98240-0468

04 03 02 • 5 4 3 2 1

Chapter One

"Faster, Marigold!"

The chestnut mare galloped across the flats outside Salt Lake City.

"Go!" I pressed my heels to her sides, wrapped my fingers in her wild tangle of mane, and urged her on, my own hair whipping about my face.

I laughed, thinking of the warm biscuits and gravy Ma would have ready when I got home. I'd give Marigold's legs a good rubdown when we got back to the farm. Already I could feel her muscles unknotting beneath my hands.

Marigold took the bit between her teeth and bolted.

"Watch out!" I screamed, hauling her head to the side, desperate to turn her so she didn't step in the —

Marigold lurched as her foot hit the rabbit hole. With a sickening *crack*, she stumbled. Down she went, her eyes wild. I sailed over her shoulder, my mouth gaping as I tried to scream. Only a harsh gargle came out as I hit the ground.

Clip-clop-clip-clop. For a moment I thought it was Marigold, trotting away without me. But the chink and jingle of harness and the rumble of a heavy cart made no sense.

I opened my eyes to the shadowy gray shapes of the orphanage sleeping room. I swear, I didn't know whether to laugh with joy because Marigold hadn't really broken her leg or weep with the knowledge that I was still at the Carson City Home for Unfortunate Girls. There would be no warm biscuits and gravy, for my mother was dead, lost in childbirth along with my tiny baby sister, Grace.

At the thought of my dear mother and sister, my eyes stung and I rolled onto my stomach and buried my face in the pillow.

Sliding my hand along the rough sheet, I felt for my penknife hidden under the pillow. All around, thirteen other girls slept, their breathing deep and even. I envied them their last moments of rest. Heaven knows, Miss Critchett would be coming around soon enough to wake us.

"Six o'clock, ladies," she'd say. Then we'd pray and Mrs. Pinweather would deliver a solemn sermon about proper deportment and the evils of gin before we would be allowed to form two smart lines and march — in silence — to the eating hall.

Breakfast was never a meal to get excited about. Porridge and weak tea filled our bellies, I suppose, but my, how I missed Ma's biscuits and bacon. Worst of all, we had to eat that paltry meal without speaking a single word. Now why, I ask you, would the good Lord have put tongues in our heads if he didn't mean for us to make good use of them?

Miss Critchett and Mrs. Pinweather saw things otherwise. Both held the opinion that excessive chatter was one of many behaviors considered pernicious. They never explained exactly what *pernicious* meant, but they made it clear that it was neither *pious* nor *conducive to the development of good moral character.*

Supposing nobody dropped dead of boredom during the morning lessons in reading, writing, and numbers, we were allowed an hour for a silent dinner before afternoon lessons in deportment and domestic studies. Those, I loathed more than anything. I'm no good at needlepoint and mending. Why should we be judged as valuable or not based on how perfectly we can stitch *Lord Bless This Home*? Nobody asked whether any of us could gentle a foal, handle a team, or start three-year-olds under saddle. At these I was as skilled as any boy, but at the orphanage it was considered most unladylike to be interested in the work of men.

Wide awake after my horrible dream about Marigold, I crept to the window and ran my fingers under the window ledge just as I had done every morning since July 8th, 1859, the day my brothers left me behind. One notch for each day of my imprisonment. *Ninety-eight. Ninety-nine.* I dug the tip of my knife into the soft wood and made a slanted mark through the previous four.

"One hundred," I whispered. One hundred days since my brothers had abandoned me. One hundred and two days since the death of my father on the wagon trail. Fifty-six days since my twelfth birthday.

I closed my eyes and pressed my forehead to the windowpane. What would Pa think of me being here and the boys going on to California? Surely that was not what Pa had in mind when, through his pain and fever, he had said, "Jackson? Will? You take care of little Joselyn, you hear?"

My throat felt funny when I thought of him lying in the back of the wagon, his face flushed, his skin dry and hot, and his wounded foot oozing and swollen so big I couldn't even see his toes.

Joselyn, I scolded myself, that's no way to remember your beloved Pa, God rest his soul. Don't dwell on such things.

Outside, two men rode past, hats pulled low and shoulders hunched against the cold. I rubbed my arms: Miss Critchett didn't believe in wasting coal while we slept. Creeping back into bed, I tugged the gray blanket up around the back of my neck. Miss Critchett didn't believe in thick blankets, either.

The one-hundredth day. Perhaps it would be different from the ninety-nine others that had come before. I wrapped the blanket more closely about me, for once eager to hear Miss Critchett's footsteps in the hall.

Chapter Two

"But, Ma'am — "

"Miss Whyte!"

I sat back down on the bench, too low to see out the window. The door burst open and Miss Critchett entered, her skirts swirling, her hands twisting together. She whispered something to Mrs. Pinweather and our teacher's hand flew to her mouth. Both women turned to stare toward the window and the other girls shifted uneasily on the benches.

"In – di – ans." I mouthed the word

to Mary Brown who sat beside me. She bit down so hard her teeth made two white lines in her bottom lip.

"Here?" she whispered.

I nodded. Outside, the street was filled with Indian men on ponies.

The two women spoke in hushed voices. Mary Brown reached for my hand.

"Ladies." Mrs. Pinweather pressed a knot of fingers against her bosom. "I implore you to remain quiet and calm. Miss Critchett and I have no means to protect you should the Indians decide to — " Her voice trailed off and Mary Brown gasped, clenching her hand around mine so tightly I nearly cried out.

Miss Critchett stepped forward. "We feel that it would not be wise to allow you to remain here at the orphanage if there is going to be trouble."

My back stiffened.

"But where shall we go?" Emily Hampton asked. Two of the younger girls at the front of the room whimpered.

"We had word Indians were coming this way. We have found safe homes in town where you will be able to stay until — "

Mrs. Pinweather faltered again and Miss Critchett added, "Until the danger of Indian attack has passed."

I closed my eyes. Mary Brown's sweaty hand was still clamped around mine. If the Indians did attack us, we would all be dead no matter where we tried to hide. There were few militiamen in Carson City to protect us. By the time reinforcements arrived ... It did not bear thinking about.

"We shall be all right," I said to Mary Brown. "Have faith. God will not let us perish."

I don't know whether I believed my own words, but if Mary Brown didn't release my hand, all my fingers would drop off and roll across the floor like little sausages. This thought was so foolish I nearly laughed aloud, but the terror in Mary's eyes made me reach over to pat her shoulder and gently ask her to let go of me instead.

"Mrs. Ormsby, this is Joselyn Whyte. Bless you for opening your home to her during this difficult time."

Mrs. Ormsby sniffed and blinked. "This is a dreadful thing, but my husband knows how to deal with the Indians. I'm certain the guilty men will be found."

I looked from Miss Critchett to Mrs. Ormsby, wondering what Mrs. Ormsby meant about guilty men.

"I certainly hope the matter will be settled quickly so you will not be too inconvenienced by Miss Whyte's time with you. The girl is a hard worker, though not especially good with needlepoint."

I bristled at the remark, though I said nothing. Instead, I lowered my eyes and studied the wooden floor beyond Mrs. Ormsby's wide skirts.

When Miss Critchett had gone, Mrs. Ormsby showed me to a small room off the kitchen where I was to stay. It did not surprise me that I was to share my room — there were three beds inside — but imagine my horror when I saw before me an Indian girl! I had never seen an Indian up close and presumed them all to be filthy savages. How wrong all my ideas about Indians would turn out to be.

"Sarah — this is Joselyn. She will stay with us for a short time until ... until the troubles have been resolved."

I expected Sarah to look angry or afraid. After all, Mrs. Ormsby was speaking of Sarah's people. Perhaps she had not understood what Mrs. Ormsby had said. But Sarah, who wore a dress not unlike my own, nodded. Her two black braids dipped and rose with her nod. She gestured to the empty bed closest to the door leading back into the kitchen.

I could not stop staring. She looked nothing like I would have expected. Her brown skin was soft-looking and clean and her black hair was so glossy it shone in the lamplight when she moved her head. Yes, she most certainly was an Indian, and yet, I did not feel afraid. Though her eyes were dark and her nose a little broader than mine, she simply looked like a girl about my age, sturdy and not at all unfriendly.

"You must not worry," she said. I started, shocked that the words coming from her mouth were spoken as clearly as if Mary Brown had said them herself. "My brother and cousin are among the men who have come to Carson City. They are friends with Major Ormsby and are here to talk of the trouble. No harm will come to anyone, your people or mine."

She seemed so certain that I wondered why everyone was so afraid.

"What trouble?" I asked. "Why are your men here?" Indian warriors rarely came to Carson City and certainly not in such numbers. "And why are you here, in this house?" For this was the most remarkable thing of all, to find an Indian girl living at Ormsby House.

Sarah smiled. "My father is the great Chief Winnemucca. Major Ormsby and my father are good friends. My father believes that we must learn the ways of the white people. And so, I have come here with my sister to learn how to live as you do and how to speak your language."

"Your sister is here, too?"

"Yes." Sarah gestured to the third bed. "We play with Lizzie, Major Ormsby's daughter. I also help with the cooking and cleaning."

At this I had to sit down on the bed by the door.

"You ask what has happened, why our men are here."

All I could do was nod and listen.

"The chiefs are here to help find the Indians who murdered two white miners."

"Your people murdered — "

Sarah raised her hand and gave me a look of disgust. "No." The tips of her braids twitched from side to side as she shook her head. "No. The white men were found with Washo arrows in their wounds. Our people are the Paiutes. Our arrows look different. My cousin, Chief Numaga, knows where to find the Washo Indians. He will ask their chief to send the guilty men so they can be punished."

"Your cousin will bring the guilty Indians here, to Carson City?"

"I told you, my people and Major Ormsby are friends. As friends, we must help make sure right is done." She tilted her head toward the dark window. "We must hurry now to help prepare the evening meal." Sarah Winnemucca, her back straight, her walk quiet but confident, moved past me and out of the room.

Nothing was ordinary about the rest of that evening. Indian men with rabbit fur robes and quivers of arrows across their backs came and went. Sarah pointed out her cousin, Numaga, a huge man with a deep chest and powerful shoulders. Like Sarah, he walked with such sureness that I had no doubt he was a great leader and brave warrior. These men were honorable, I told myself. They had come to Carson City to help Major Ormsby, not to attack those of us living peacefully in town.

After dinner, Major Ormsby smoked and talked with Chief Numaga in the parlor. Then, later in the evening, the chief prepared to leave. On his way out he said something to Sarah in their language and Sarah rose up on her toes with excitement. She turned to me and said, "Would you like to see a war dance?"

Mrs. Ormsby, standing in the doorway of the parlor, drew in a sharp breath. "I scarcely think that would be — "

Sarah stood even taller. "Chief Numaga has no quarrel with your people. He makes his men ready for travel at dawn to find the criminal Washos."

A war dance! "What's a war dance like?" I asked.

Sarah smiled. "I have never seen one."

My mouth dropped open. Surely she was lying.

"My people are peaceful. They will not fight unless forced to by trouble brought upon them by others."

Mrs. Ormsby's arms were crossed. Her face was tight.

A man rushed into the front hall where we stood, banging the door open.

He shouted, "Them braves is dancing! They got a big fire in the square."

Sure enough, through the open door we could see the glow of a bonfire out in the street. Without waiting for Mrs. Ormsby to gather her senses, Sarah snatched two shawls from the coat rack, took my hand, and pulled me outside.

I gasped in the cold air and pulled the shawl closer about my shoulders. The night was already so cold that I hardly dared think of what the winter ahead might bring.

Sarah and I ran toward the blazing fire. It seemed all of Carson City had gathered to watch the Paiutes chanting and stamp-stamp-stamping around their fire. At first, more than one man held his rifle at the ready. But as the dancers continued, it grew clear that this was a celebration and that the men meant us no harm.

We stayed and watched for a long time, huddled together for warmth, the glow of the fire casting long shadows into the street behind us. Finally, the dancing stopped and Sarah and I walked, arms linked, back to Ormsby House.

When we arose the next morning, Chief Numaga and all of his warriors were gone.

Though the immediate danger seemed to have passed, I stayed at Ormsby House. Sarah and I worked from before first light, cooking and cleaning. She was excellent company and I soon came to think of her as a good friend. I saw little of Sarah's younger sister who spent most of her time with young Lizzie Ormsby.

Many men came and went. Most of those who stayed for a night or two in the boarding rooms upstairs were miners or settlers, though occasionally soldiers or Indian agents stopped by. The most interesting of them all were the Pony Express riders. They rode into town at breakneck speed on beautiful, fast horses, mailbags slung across their saddles. Taking turns riding sections of the trail, they carried the mail clear across the country from Missouri to

California. They must have been going near as quick as birds to get the mail delivered as fast as they did — in as little as ten days, when all went well.

For the most part they were good men, many not much more than boys, who stayed away from cards and rum and left the women alone. A couple of times I watched the quick change of men and horses at the Carson City station across the way and wished I could somehow slip into a mailbag and send myself to California.

When I told Sarah of my foolish idea, she laughed and said, "A job won't be done unless you do it yourself." I told her she sounded like my pa and she laughed even louder. Then she told me that she herself had traveled to California and that if I were so inclined I should make arrangements.

At the time I thought she spoke in jest, for I did not know how a young girl like me could travel so great a distance alone. But the seed had been planted. With time, that seed would grow into a plan.

Chapter Three

When the Paiutes returned to Carson City, they brought with them the Washo chief and three young Washo men with their wives, mothers, and sisters.

"These are the guilty men," the Washo chief said. The young men were promptly arrested, their arms pulled behind their backs and tied tightly at the wrists.

A crowd gathered to see the Indians and many of the white people hollered rude things at them. The Indian women who had come with their men cried and wailed. One old woman shouted at Major Ormsby who was pointing at the jailhouse.

"What are they saying?" I asked Sarah.

"They say the men are innocent, that their chief only brought them here so the Washos did not have to make war with the Paiutes."

Two men with rifles came toward the crowd and, seeing them, the three Washo men shrieked in terror. They struggled against the white men who held them. First one, and then the other two, broke free and ran.

Everyone was screaming and shouting. The two men with rifles raised their guns and fired again and again. The three Indian men fell onto the icy ground, blood pouring from their wounds. The women cried out in horror and rushed to their sides, howling with grief.

Sarah turned to Mrs. Ormsby and said, in a voice so quiet it made me shiver, "I believe those women. I don't think those men were guilty."

"I won't hear such nonsense. My husband knows what he is doing."

Sarah said nothing to this but turned

her back on the hideous scene before us and walked away.

A short time after that, her cousin, Chief Numaga, came to take Sarah and her sister from Major Ormsby's house. I missed her more than I would have imagined. But part of me was also envious. Sarah's father, Chief Winnemucca, her grandfather, a man they called Old Truckee, and her cousin, Chief Numaga, would never abandon her the way my own heartless brothers had done. Who would rescue me?

The mood of Carson City turned dark. Blood had been spilled on our streets. For many days stains could be seen where the Washo men had fallen. When we heard that white men, robbers, had been the ones to murder the miners for their money, I thought of Sarah and hoped she and her people, and the Washo people, too, could forgive the men of Carson City for shooting the innocent Washo men.

Things went from bad to worse as the coldest winter anyone could remember settled in. With Sarah gone, Mrs. Ormsby could not manage without my help. I stayed on at Ormsby House.

Long after Christmas had come and gone, we heard that the Paiutes had attacked the Williams brothers' place, burned it to the ground, and killed both brothers and several others besides. Why would they have done such a thing? It made no sense at all.

When Major Ormsby heard of the attack on Williams Station, he was furious. "It's time we teach those double-crossing Paiutes a lesson," he declared. Word spread like wildfire. Over the next two days several dozen men gathered downstairs, drank whiskey, and made plans for revenge. Mrs. Ormsby and I brought the men steaming bowls of soup and slabs of bread. The men made plans to ride toward Pyramid Lake where Sarah's people lived.

"We'll show them Indians what happens when they attack a white man," a round fellow with gray hair said as he raised his glass.

My blood chilled in my veins as I thought of Sarah, her sister, and the rest of her family. There must have been a reason for the attack on Williams Station. I knew Sarah well enough to know that her people would not have attacked without reason. The Williams brothers must have done something terrible. Everyone knew they were nothing but trouble. They cheated everybody — whites and Indians alike — and had more enemies than anyone else I knew.

But the drunken men at Ormsby House did not care to remember these facts. At dawn the next morning, the whole lot of them set off riding horses thin from poor feed and a long winter.

When we heard some days later that there had been a terrible battle near Pyramid Lake during which our men had been ambushed by the Paiutes, I was not sure what to think. Many white men had been killed. One of the dead was Major Ormsby. Mrs. Ormsby and Lizzie were near blind with distress. Behind closed curtains, they clutched at each other and wept. In the quiet of that morning, the house was still save for the sounds of their misery.

On the day that we heard the terrible news about the defeat of the men from Carson City, I was sent back to the orphanage. Together, we all waited to see what might happen next.

The settlers and townsfolk wasted no time. Immediately, they began to plan another attack on the Indians. Though it was May, snow continued to fall and I found myself wondering whether God was punishing the people for all the killing.

Though Miss Critchett and Mrs. Pinweather tried hard to bring some order to our days, none of us could concentrate on our lessons or needlepoint. Every loud noise outside made us jump. We were at war with the Paiutes and none of us knew when their warriors might ride back into Carson City, this time to attack us as they had attacked Major Ormsby and his men.

No matter how I tried to busy myself, I never felt safe. I often thought of Sarah and worried that she would be killed in the battle that was sure to follow. Sarah's words about going to California came to me as I lay in my bed each night. California seemed so far away, so safe. Finally, I decided to make some arrangements to get myself out of Carson City. From that moment on my mind did not rest.

How would I get away? Where could I get my hands on some money? Even if I could somehow buy a stage ticket, surely someone would ask questions of a girl travelling alone. They'd bring me back and I'd be stuck here again.

The whole plan of my escape came to me in small pieces, like patches in a quilt. The first piece to fall into place was David Morton's cap.

The Home for Unfortunate Girls employed a porter by the name of Mr. Morton who had a son called David. David had ears so big they might have belonged to a mule. He was close to my age and helped his father with the chores: chopping wood, clearing snow, and shoveling coal.

David always pulled his cap down so low over his ears you could hardly tell who was under it. If someone else put on David's cap and pulled it way down like he did, it would make a pretty good disguise. 'Course, it wouldn't work for a girl — unless — unless the girl cut off her hair.

I wrapped the end of one of my long braids around my finger and looked down at my dress and pinafore. If a girl cut off her hair and wore boy's clothes, maybe, just maybe, she could pass as a boy, particularly if the girl was tall and bony and pockmarked like me.

Not long after that I saw my chance to take David's hat.

The nights were still bitterly cold when a new delivery of coal arrived for the hulking furnace in the cellar. David's father shoveled the coal into the chute leading down into the cellar. David's job was to move the coal back to make room for more. It wasn't quite high enough for him to stand up in the cellar, so before he went in he hung his hat on a peg by the door. Poor fool. It was no trouble to take his cap from the peg and tuck it up under my pinafore until I could get back to my room to hide it.

I didn't feel real good when his pa boxed his ears for his careless ways, but I didn't feel bad enough to give the hat back, either. After all, David was lucky to have a pa, even one with a temper.

It wasn't right to steal, but, the way I figured, if the Good Lord hadn't meant for me to have the cap he wouldn't have put the idea in my head to take it and most certainly wouldn't have left it hanging right there on the peg as plain as day.

A pair of trousers was harder to come by. At about this time Miss Critchett got the idea of taking in washing as well as the mending we already did.

My job was to crank the big handle of the wringer to squeeze the water out of the sopping wet laundry. Another girl, Kathleen, worked with me. We both grew strong cranking that handle.

Sometimes, Kathleen would look at me with her droopy eyes and say, "I bet we could make a fortune in the gold fields if we ran a laundry."

Then we wouldn't talk for a long time because we were both thinking about the gold fields. Always, when the afternoon's work was done, I felt a little bit sad because I so longed to know what had become of my brothers. But I only stayed sad for a short time before I grew spitting mad at the two of them for leaving me behind. It was best not to think of them at all, for such black thoughts as I had served only to darken my soul.

One laundry day I dropped a pair of trousers right into the mud.

"Now look what you've done," Kathleen said.

"I'll take 'em back inside," I said, and hurried into the kitchen.

The big washtub stood in the middle of the kitchen floor half-filled with murky water. Two kettles heated on the wood stove, but the girls were not there.

After a long moment I tucked the pants under my pinafore and rushed up to the sleeping room. There, I pried loose a wide floorboard from under my bed and stretched the trousers out in the small space so they could dry. I pressed the board back and hurried outside where Kathleen cranked the handle by herself.

"Seems it took a long time to take them pants inside."

I wiped my hands on my pinafore and took hold of the handle.

"I had to stop at the privy on my way back," I said, hoping that would satisfy her.

It seemed to. We worked for the rest of the afternoon without saying much, cranking the handle of the ringer around and around. We hung the damp clothes from the washline until a whole army of trousers marched before the breeze.

I waited nearly three more weeks before I hid a shirt behind the wood-pile when Kathleen's back was turned. Later, I fetched it and stuffed it into the same space beneath the bed where

I had hidden the trousers and the cap.

Finally, nearly ten months to the day after my brothers had left me behind, I was ready to borrow the shears from the sewing room and put the final part of my plan into action. By then, I was a full head taller than Miss Critchett and not quite thirteen years of age.

Chapter Four

The evening I borrowed the shears, I was so petrified that I nearly changed my mind about running away. Even when all the other girls were breathing evenly, I forced myself to keep still under the blanket for a while longer, just to be sure.

All I had to do to steady my nerves was imagine another year of stitching samplers and lugging wet laundry while I waited for a war to happen right in Carson City. There had been another big fight near Pyramid Lake, this time with soldiers from as far away as California. As near as I could tell, nobody won and nobody lost, though men on both sides lost their lives. In the end, the Paiutes headed deeper into the hills and the settlers came back to the towns and homesteads.

I hid under my covers for a long while before I took hold of the end of one of my thick braids, scarcely daring to breathe. *Snip*, it was done. Too late to stop, I snipped off the other braid.

My hair fell about my ears in a square, short cut like a boy's. By stretching my arm under my bed I could just reach my fingers to the crack in the floor and slowly pry up the loose board, praying it wouldn't creak. I reached underneath for the stolen trousers and shirt, pulled them under my thin blanket, and wriggled into them. My, didn't it feel strange to be wearing a man's pants! When I reached up to touch what was left of my hair, I felt stranger still.

I tucked my nightdress and my braids under the loose board. Then, with the moon spilling cold light across the wood

floor, I crept from my bed, pulled David's cap low over my ears, and slipped along the hall to the sewing room to replace the shears.

"Oh!" I gasped aloud as I caught sight of my reflection in the looking glass. For a moment I thought David was in the sewing room with me and I clapped my hand over my mouth to stop myself from screaming. But when I touched my other hand to my cap, the person in the glass touched his cap, too, so it was me all right. I turned to the side and then back the other way. A boy. I looked like a boy for certain.

There was no time to waste admiring myself. I tiptoed down to the kitchen. Once, I stepped on a loose floorboard and the creaks sounded as loud as a baby's wailing. I stood stock-still and held my breath. But the place remained quiet save for the *tick-tock-tick* of the big grandfather clock in the front entry hall.

At last I reached the kitchen door. As I struggled to lift the stiff latch, it occurred to me I'd best take some kind of food along. I helped myself to half a loaf of bread and pushed aside my guilty feelings. All things considered, it was a small enough contribution for the orphanage to make to the rest of my life.

Just like that, I was outside making my way through the dark streets of Carson City. I had to find a place to hide as soon as possible because, come morning, they would be looking for me. I dodged from shadow to shadow, keeping my eyes down and staying out of the way of the few men who staggered along the main street.

Trouble was, I had no idea where to go. My plans had only extended to escape from the orphanage walls. Ormsby House was out of the question. Mrs. Ormsby would send me right back. The night was cool but the breeze carried the smells of early summer. In the distance, a dog barked. From somewhere in the hills, the eerie wails of coyotes answered.

I skirted around the edges of town and when the dawn began to break I took refuge in a deep pile of straw in the back corner of the stable behind the freight station. I slept uneasily, jumping at each rustle in the straw. Once I sat up, convinced someone was trying to saw a hole in the wall, but it was only the wind working a loose board back and forth.

My growling belly woke me. Every part of my skin scratched and prickled from all the hay. All I could think of was how much I wanted to go back, even if that meant begging for forgiveness from Miss Critchett.

Then I remembered something my pa always used to say, Don't never think on an empty stomach.

Gnawing on the last of the bread, I tried my best to ignore the uneasy squeezing deep in my belly. What had I gone and done? Without a penny to my name I would never be able to get to California. Heck, as it stood, I couldn't even buy me another loaf of bread.

"Here he comes!" someone shouted from just outside the barn. I eased back into the shadows.

Horse's hooves pounded toward the barn at a gallop. They stopped outside and I heard men talking and the heavy breathing of a horse that had been run hard.

"Here, let me walk him." The tired horse's breathing moved farther from the barn.

"Any trouble on your run?"

"Some Indian fires in the hills, but no trouble."

"Aye — those militia patrols are doing a good job of keeping the trail open. Bad news, though — the rider didn't show. I heard tell he's been drinking again."

"So, I got to go on?"

"'Fraid so. Be a bonus in it for you, though."

The rider gave a short laugh. "Assumin' I'll be in any shape at the other end of the ride to claim it."

I heard the smack of leather and the uneasy movement of a fresh horse.

"Up you go, then. Godspeed."

With a grunt, the rider settled onto the new horse. "Gee-yap!" He was off, his horse's hooves drumming a rapid departure from Carson City.

"We need more men like him," a voice said and I realized the second man had returned with the first horse. Its breathing had slowed a little.

"Aye. That we do. I have a notice posted. With any luck we'll attract some fresh blood."

"With any luck, yes. I'll cool Big Sam out a little longer. Then, how about some coffee?"

"Sounds mighty good to me," the first man said.

For the next little while all I could hear was the slow, even sound of the horse being walked back and forth outside. When the hoof beats came straight toward the barn, I scurried out of sight. I had just enough time to tug a couple of empty feed sacks over top of me before the door opened.

"Good boy, Sammy. Here you go."

Hay rustled and the man left, the latch clicking shut behind him.

I moved quietly to where a tall, black horse was tethered. Big Sam was a handsome animal. He steamed slightly in the cool air of the barn as he munched his hay.

The men sounded like they were with the Pony Express. It didn't take long for me to find the notice they had spoken of. It was posted clear as day on the front wall of the freight company.

Wanted: Young, skinny, wiry fellows.
Not over 18. Must be willing to risk death daily.
Orphans preferred.
Wages $25 per week.
Inquire within.

Twenty-five dollars a week? That was a small fortune! With work like that it wouldn't take long to save enough money to get to California. A coach ticket from Carson City cost a little more than a hundred dollars. Then I'd need enough put aside to pay for room and board and maybe hire me a guide to take me to the gold fields to find my brothers.

I leaned forward and read the notice again. It sounded so exciting. I glanced up and down the street and read the notice one more time.

Orphans preferred. Well, that was me, sure enough.

It was horses, it was riding, and they wanted skinny boys. Sure I was skinny, but did I look enough like a boy to get the job? If I did, the work would get me out of town in a hurry. I looked up the road again. Then, without pondering further on the ifs and maybes, I stepped forward and knocked on the freight office door.

"C'mon in."

I pushed the door open and stepped inside. The office wasn't large, but it was warm. Two men looked at me over steaming mugs of coffee.

"What can I do for you, son?"

I ducked my head, cleared my throat, pushed my voice low, and mumbled, "Saw the notice."

The man who had spoken stood up and thrust his hand toward me. "You've come to the right place. Name is Bolivar Roberts with the Pony Express. So happens we're looking to replace a few riders in Utah Territory."

I nodded and he went on.

"How old are you, boy?" Mr. Roberts asked.

"Sixteen — sir," I said, forcing my voice deep into my chest and drawing myself up straight and tall, proud for once of my gangly height. "Been riding since I was eight years old with my pa who is now dead, which makes me an orphan."

"What's your name?" Mr. Roberts asked.

I hadn't thought of that. "Ahhh ... Jo — "

He raised an eyebrow and gave me a hard look.

"Jo Wh-whyte," I stammered.

"Where you from?"

"Salt Lake City, sir. In the valley. We had ourselves a ranch there, sir."

"Utah Territory is where we need riders."

"Yes, sir."

"Hard territory. Some trouble between here and Salt Lake. Indians."

"Yes, sir. I got friends among the Paiutes." I hoped Sarah would still think of me as her friend.

Mr. Roberts grunted. "I do believe the worst is over. The Paiutes agreed to keep to their land and not attack and we've agreed to leave 'em alone. Not much worth having in the desert where they live anyway."

Standing there in the small office wanting that Pony Express job more than anything, I kept my peace.

"Besides, they're building a fort on the river — Fort Churchill. When it's done, two thousand men will live there. That should keep them Indians in line should they forget their danged manners."

I bit the inside of my cheek and nodded again.

"I'm short a couple of riders between Ruby and Egan Canyon. Do you know the territory?"

"Yes, sir. More or less." Hadn't I traveled along that very trail with Will and Jackson?

"That's fine, Joe Whyte. Be here at

first light tomorrow and Smokey McPhail will ride with you up to Ruby Valley."

I nodded, scarcely able to keep from crying, I was so happy.

"Before you go anywhere, you got to swear this oath."

I nodded again. I would have sworn anything to be leaving Carson City and earning enough money so I could be on my way to California. Mr. Roberts pushed two objects across the desk: a Bible small enough to fit in a jacket pocket and a pistol.

"You'll need both of these," he said and tapped the Bible with his knuckle. I placed my fingertips on the leather cover and repeated everything Mr. Roberts said.

"Mail first. Pony second. Rider third. The mail must get through," I added for good measure.

"You got that right. Our business is built on trust, speed, and reliability. Sometimes we ship valuable documents, important news, and occasionally, cash deliveries. We count on our riders to get the mail through no matter what."

I swore that I'd uphold the ideals of the Pony Express Company — no drinking, no gambling, and no unlawful deeds. I glanced down at my stolen shirt and pants. If I could do this job, my stealing days would be over for good.

With the advance Mr. Roberts offered me, I bought gloves, a hat and jacket, and a leather holster. Though it must have seemed a mite rude, I never once removed my cap inside for fear I would be recognized. Instead, I kept it right down over my eyes and mumbled my answers, always careful to keep my voice gruff and low as I made my purchases.

Once I thought I saw Mrs. Pinweather hurrying along the road, and I ducked between two wagons and counted to one hundred before venturing out again.

Early in the afternoon I took my bundles, a fresh loaf of bread, and some hard cheese back to the barn and hid myself away in the darkest corner.

That night I slept like an old dog. At dawn I tugged the collar of my new jacket up, felt my pockets for my Bible and the knife my pa had given me, patted my holster, and marched around to the front of the freight office.

This time when I reached the office door, I walked right in.

Chapter Five

Two men, Mr. Bolivar Roberts and a younger man I didn't recognize, sat at the table.

"Mornin', Joe," Mr. Roberts said.

I nodded.

"This here's Smokey McPhail."

The man, who looked to be about the same age as my oldest brother, William, raised his tin mug toward me.

"Smokey will take you on up to Ruby Valley, where you'll start your first run. It'll take you 'bout three days to make the trip."

Smokey rocked his chair back and studied me. I blushed. He had guessed my secret; I just knew it.

"I got a question for you," he said and I shifted from foot to foot, certain he was going to ask me if I was really a boy.

"You ain't yet sixteen, are you?"

I let out my breath and coughed, staring at my feet so I wouldn't have to look him in the eye.

"Near enough."

"No need to mumble. I can see you ain't shaving yet."

I put my hand to my chin. I wasn't likely to start shaving any time soon, either.

"No matter. If you can ride, I ain't going to complain. None of the men on this job is much older than you."

I coughed again and risked a glance at Mr. Roberts.

"Have yourself a biscuit and some coffee and then you'd best be going."

I took a warm biscuit and stuffed my mouth full. If I was eating, I couldn't be talking, and if I wasn't talking, I couldn't be giving myself away.

Soon as I was done, the three of us headed to the corral out back. We leaned over the top rail watching the half dozen horses eating their hay. Big Sam was among them and I wondered if I'd be riding him.

"Take Sheba and Rocko," Mr. Roberts said indicating a flea-bitten, gray mare and a bay gelding.

I tried to ignore the fact that both men were watching me as we readied the horses, looking to see just how familiar I was with working around the animals. That much, at least, I wasn't worried about. I'd helped my pa with the stock for as long as I could remember. Pa used to say some folks had the touch with horses and he was right proud his daughter was one of them.

We mounted up and set out at a brisk trot for Dayton. Smokey tipped his hat at the stationmaster but we didn't stop. We rode past Miller's Station and on to Fort Churchill where we changed horses. The fort bustled with dozens of men hard at work building the stockade and bunkhouses.

Smokey didn't seem to mind that I didn't care to talk much. He filled the time by talking non-stop himself, about his ma back in Boston, some of the rides he'd made with the Pony Express, and before that with the mule trains carrying mail to California.

"Horses are a damned sight easier to get along with," he said with a grin. "Mules are too darned smart for their own good." Even though he talked a lot his eyes never stopped scanning the trail ahead, wary of ambushes. The worst sections were those that passed right through stands of aspen trees. If the way had been straight, it would have been easier, but the path twisted this way and that and the trees and brush were so tight together we couldn't see far ahead at all. In most places the trail was so narrow that Smokey had to ride on ahead and then the skin on my back fairly crawled. I kept looking back over my shoulder to see if anyone was coming up behind us. We wasted no time at all in those trees, that's for certain.

Cantering out along the trail past Fort Churchill, we made good time to Buckland Station. On and on we rode, changing horses once more before we reached Shelly Creek shortly after dark. There we fed and watered the horses before fixing a simple supper in a small, rough cabin that served as the stationhouse.

"'Course, when you're carrying the mail, there ain't no stopping at night," he said. "You ride by the light of the moon and appreciate real fast just how good horses can see in the dark."

I appreciated the dark all right when I excused myself to take care of my private business behind a clump of sagebrush before turning in. There weren't no such thing as a privy where we stopped. At night every sound seemed close by and the moment I was finished I hiked up my trousers and hurried to join the others in the cabin. I was some glad to close that door behind me and crawl into a bunk.

Two miners and several militiamen played cards. The two losers would have to sit outside all night, rifles at the ready. Even knowing we had men outside keeping watch, I didn't exactly lose myself to happy dreaming that night.

The next day was much the same and so was the one following as we headed toward Ruby Valley. I always felt uneasy. Even when we were supposed to sleep, I tossed and turned and fretted so much it was hardly worth the effort of lying down in the first place.

Each day as we rode, Smokey told me all kinds of useful things about the express company, the horses we would be using, and the way things were run. "Finest horses around, I'll say that," Smokey said. "Fast and fit and grain-fed. They can go real quick for ten, twelve miles or so. Then you change onto a fresh set of legs and keep on moving up the trail."

Smokey explained the route, the stations where I'd stop to change horses, and how long it would take me to ride from Ruby Valley on to Butte Station or Egan Canyon. He told me landmarks to watch for since he would take me only as far as Ruby Valley and my first run would be onwards to Butte. It was a good thing he tended to say things over and over since my head was so weary and muddled I could hardly follow a word.

In the cabin at Diamond Springs on our last morning together, Smokey blew on his coffee and nodded toward a steaming cup on the rough plank table.

"Coffee?"

I nodded and jammed my hat on harder. If I kept my hat on low, and my voice quiet, I might just keep fooling folks.

"Arbuckle's. Only the best for our riders."

The dark burn of the coffee in my throat was heavenly.

We continued east on fresh horses that day and made excellent time to Ruby Valley. At mid-morning we rode up to the station house and stock corrals where we found a dozen or so men working around several small buildings.

"Colonel Rogers, this here is Joe," Smokey said as I climbed down from my horse. The colonel held out his hand and we shook.

"Welcome," he said. "Call me Uncle Billy like most folks do."

After we put the horses away, Uncle Billy showed me into the stationhouse. "It's a short run for you tomorrow — just to Butte. Should be able to do it in three hours with horse changes at Mountain Springs and Cherry Bend."

He made it sound like nothing, but, to be honest, I felt a bit faint thinking about galloping so many miles of trail, all before noon, all on my own. I was surely grateful that my first run would be during daylight hours, but worried that I might not remember what Smokey had told me. What if I turned down a wrong canyon and ran headlong into a bunch of Paiutes who might not have heard about the agreement to stop fighting? Even worse, maybe I'd stumble on some Washos wanting revenge for the men who'd been shot in Carson City. My single pistol wouldn't do me much good. I needed to practice. Then I felt terrible. What if I accidentally shot Sarah's cousin, Chief Numaga, or her brother, Natchez? Sarah would hate me then, no matter what my reasons might have been for opening fire.

"You up for chopping some wood?" Uncle Billy asked.

"Yes, sir," I said, happy for the distraction.

Chop. Whack. The wood was dry and split neatly, the pieces flying to either side of the stump. It didn't take long before my arms ached something fierce — even hauling wet laundry hadn't made me strong enough for wood-chopping.

I'd split maybe twenty logs and my arms felt as if stones were tied to the ends of them.

"Want me to spell you off?"

I was so startled the ax missed the stump completely. It swung toward my leg in a long, deadly arc. How I managed to jerk the ax and my leg away from each other I'll never know.

"What in the name of — " I dropped

the ax and whirled to face whoever had come up behind me. "You could have killed me."

"Now hold on just a minute. I was merely — "

We glared at each other.

The boy was no taller than I was, but he was stockier. Everything about him looked sturdy. He wore his trousers tucked into his leather boots and his heavy shirt flapped loosely. It looked like it had been many, many weeks since soap and water had come close to his thick, black hair.

"Bart Ridley," he said, sticking his hand out at me. "With the mail service."

"Jo," I replied. "Me too."

"Better watch how you swing that ax, Joe, or someone's gonna' git hurt."

I stared at the ax where it lay in the dirt by the stump.

"You don't got to do it all yourself. Why, when I first got this job I thought as how I had to be as strong as the older men, you know — "

I nodded my head ever so slightly

and didn't stop Bart when he picked up the ax to chop. When it was my turn again I swung the ax as hard as I could. Dang it all if I didn't feel a mite proud when Bart Ridley grunted, impressed, when my wood split into four, not just two, even pieces.

Chapter Six

That night I fell dead asleep near as soon as I lay down in my bunk. Even the talking of the men and the creaking of the bunks as they came to bed didn't rouse me from my slumber. Pa used to say that the doomed don't dream. I tried not to think about what it meant when my sleep was deep and quiet without even a nightmare to save my soul.

Uncle Billy shook me out of bed before dawn. I sat close as I could to the big, stone fireplace and filled my belly with coffee and grits.

"Come on out when you're done," Uncle Billy said and banged the door behind him. I pulled on my boots and spurs, tugged my hat down over my ears, and touched the gun nestled against my hip.

Well before the eastbound rider was due to arrive, I joined Uncle Billy outside. Bart Ridley was already waiting with my horse, a lanky sorrel mustang called Flame.

"Hey, boy," I said, smoothing my hand along the horse's neck. I took care to avoid touching Bart's hand where he held the reins even though I was wearing my calfskin gloves. If he touched my hand, would he know I was a girl?

Flame pushed his nose into my ribs and I felt the familiar puff of a horse's warm breath, recognized the kindness in his soft, brown eyes. I rubbed his neck and smiled. It sure felt good to be near horses once again. How had I managed to keep my senses about me during those long months when I lived at Ormsby House and at the orphanage?

This was no pleasure ride, I reminded myself. Flame and I had a job to do.

I readied myself to mount up so I could ride off faster, but Uncle Billy shook his head and put his hand on my shoulder to stop me. I flinched away from the touch, one foot still in the stirrup.

"Not yet, Joe. You gotta' help with the mochila."

Of course. The mailbags had to go on over the saddle before I could climb aboard. My face burned.

"Don't matter," Uncle Billy said. "You won't be wet behind the ears for long."

A cloud of dust stirred in the distance. Flame's ears tipped forward and from far off we could hear shouts, whoops, and hollers.

"Trouble?" I asked, thinking maybe robbers were chasing the rider.

"Not likely," Uncle Billy said. He spat a string of tobacco into the dirt and wiped the back of his hand across his chin. "You'd best call out just as loud when you come into Mountain Springs so they'll be ready for you."

The horse and rider grew bigger and then the dust swirled around us. The men shouted greetings and instructions as they held the sweating horse, tore the mochila from the saddle, and threw it onto Flame's back.

"Up you get, Joe," Billy said as he lifted the flap covering the only unlocked pouch. The other three, locked tight, contained the mail.

Flame quivered beneath me, ready to fly off the moment I asked.

"Hold on, there — " Uncle Billy scribbled the time the eastbound rider had arrived, checked his watch again, and wrote down a second number. He gave me a wink as he slipped the paper back into the pouch. "The mail's been stopped one minute and twenty seconds," he said. "That's more than long enough." He slapped Flame on the rump and the horse leaped forward as if shot from a cannon.

The sudden movement caught me off guard and for one horrible moment I thought my career as a Pony Express rider was over before it started.

"Hang on!" Uncle Billy shouted after me and Bart hooted with laughter.

Somehow, with a fistful of mane and every ounce of strength I possessed, I pulled myself back into the middle of the saddle, and settled in for the long ride ahead.

Flame had made the run before. He tore out along the trail heading up the valley. I glanced behind me but couldn't see much for all the dust.

Hanging onto the saddle horn with one hand and the reins with the other, I found my balance on Flame's back. He wasn't a big horse, but he was quick and sure-footed.

We weren't even clear of the valley before Flame and I began to understand each other. Some horses are heavy and sluggish, others cautious, others bold. The sorrel mustang was sensitive — I needed only to touch my heels to his sides and he bounded forward.

As we neared a bend in the trail I sat deeper in the saddle and he checked his speed and navigated the turn smoothly, his powerful haunches driving from behind, his mouth soft to the bit.

There's nothing like a fast ride on a good horse to free your thoughts, set your heart thumping, and some-times even bring a tear to your eye. Sure enough, as we crested a little hill, my eyes filled with tears. I was no longer riding hell-bent-for-leather carrying the mail. No, I was back at the end of summer two years ago riding Pa's stallion, Antonio.

"Go!" Pa had yelled, his fist punching the air. "Go, Jossie! Go!"

The tears streamed over my cheeks as I remembered the race at the fair when Antonio had galloped over the finish line. Pa had beamed at me and said, "We'll get a good price for those foals of his."

Mr. Blaine had come by soon after and Pa had said, "See? Even little Joselyn, a mere slip of a girl, can handle this magnificent animal. His foals are all fine horses with soo-peer-ior dispositions."

It worked, as it usually did. Those weanlings sold at a price that made Pa grin from ear to ear.

I wiped my cheeks with my sleeve. Don't think about him, I told myself. Think about where you are and what you are doing. Hadn't Pa always said, A man whose mind wanders on the job ain't on the job at all?

Before me, the sun rose above the mountains, bathing the peaks in a curious dry light. Flame was blowing hard and I slowed him so he could catch his breath. He stretched his neck forward and down and I knew he appreciated the chance to loosen the tight muscles in his back. We trotted along, the saddle creaking with each step. Flame's neck was dark with sweat and his breath came in short puffs. The ground began to slope down again, falling away before Flame's nimble feet.

"Oh, Pa," I said with a moan. "Pa, why'd you have to go and leave me?"

Back on level ground, I urged Flame into a canter.

No, I thought, slapping my gloved

hand on my thigh. It wasn't Pa who'd left me. It was my darned brothers. 'Course, if it weren't for those two I wouldn't have been carrying the mail all by myself, either. And, I wouldn't have met Sarah.

I chewed on that thought for awhile as we followed the trail along the side of a creek. Flame had slowed down again and I had to urge him on, hissing into his ear and squeezing my boots to his sides.

Up ahead, half a mile or so, I saw smoke rising from the chimney of Mountain Springs station.

"Git up, Flame. Go on! Your dinner's waiting." I scooped my hat off my head and whacked him on his rump.

"Haalloooo!" I jammed my hat back on and squinted to see two figures and a horse emerge from behind the low building. The waiting horse whinnied and Flame's ears twitched.

We slid to a stop in front of the cabin at Mountain Springs and I half jumped, half fell to the ground, my legs wobbly.

"Jo," I said.

"Trail's clear?" the stationkeeper asked, not concerned that I could hardly stand. If all the other riders got off and back on with no trouble, then so would I. I straightened up.

"Yup. No problems."

"Very good. Hope you don't have no trouble from here on."

As he talked, the stationkeeper pulled the mochila from Flame's back and threw it across a big roan's saddle.

"This is Bear. Faster than he looks." The horse was big-boned and lanky, with a soft expression about the face.

The second man had already led Flame away to walk him until he had cooled down. I stood at Bear's head, rubbing the horse's face, gulping down the mug of coffee the other man had handed me. The new horse puffed warm breath against my neck and I turned and blew gently into his nostrils. Pa had told me once that the Indians greeted their horses that way because that's how horses greet each other.

Bear puffed back at me and I grinned,

forgetting for a moment how badly my legs ached.

"Sixty-four minutes. Not bad for a first ride from Ruby."

Sixty-four minutes? If he'd said sixty-four hours I would have believed him.

Still, when he nodded up at the saddle I handed him my half-empty cup and climbed aboard, using Bear's mane and the saddle horn to heave myself all the way up.

The stationmaster jotted down the exact time we had taken to switch horses. "Two-o'-four. A bit slow here at the station. Git going."

And off we went, charging down the track leading to Cherry Bend some ten miles away.

Bear's gallop strides must have been full twice as long as spunky little Flame's. Soon we drew even with the big dead pine at the bend in the trail. I looked back just in time to catch a last glance of the station. "Big dead pine just past Mountain Springs," Smokey had said. "Turn slightly south and then pick up the trail again a quarter mile on."

Almost without thought I adjusted to the bigger horse's different movement, keeping my back and hips loose so as not to work against him. In turn, Bear lengthened his stride even more and dropped his head. I patted his neck and an ear twitched back toward me, listening.

"Good boy," I said.

Once again I was alone with a good horse and my thoughts. As we galloped on, my thoughts grew as sticky as the mud on this part of the trail. Difference was, I could dodge around the worst of the muck, but I couldn't do a danged thing about what I was thinking.

I'd been lucky so far, sure enough, but the men at the stations along the trail only cared about their pocket watches and keeping the mail moving. What would happen during my days of rest between runs? The men would have time to get to know me then. Somebody was sure to notice that I didn't walk quite right, or that I had no Adam's apple and really didn't need to shave at all. Ever.

Bear thundered along, carrying me closer to the next change of horses at Cherry Bend. We were soon covered with mud and the horse was tiring quickly because of the poor footing. Without Bear under me, both the mail and I would be in deep trouble.

"Whoa, now," I said, stopping him so I could dismount to let him slither down a steep hillside without my weight in the saddle.

Once at the bottom, I scrambled back up as fast as I could and urged Bear on. Pa would have been proud, though Ma would have thought her only daughter a fool — an ungodly fool out in the middle of nowhere, instead of learning how to stitch samplers.

"My Lord! Bear!" I grabbed for the saddle horn when Bear gave a great leap sideways, nearly losing me in a puddle. A jackrabbit bounded away and I cursed the horse for being so foolish as to think a rabbit could have hurt him. Then I cursed myself for not paying attention.

After that, I watched more carefully. Anything could be hiding in the bushes along the side of the trail. Coyotes. Wolves. Bandits. Miners mad with the fever. Indians at war. The more I thought about what might lurk around every bend, the more frightened I became.

"I'm real sorry, sir," I'd say to the stationmaster at Butte. "I won't be doing another run. I just remembered a very important meeting in California with my brothers." Or, "You see I can't possibly keep this job because I'm a girl."

That would give them a turn! Dang it, Joselyn. Stop thinking that way! You ain't stopping what you've started.

Pa didn't like quitters. I was going to the gold fields whether or not I ever found my no-good brothers. Besides, there was the small problem of the money I had to pay back for the gear I'd bought. A man's only as good as the debts he pays, Pa used to say. Pa wouldn't have quit before he paid back every penny and neither would I.

Chapter Seven

The sun rose higher and higher. About mid-morning, maybe a mile before Cherry Bend, I saw four wagons and about a dozen men and boys on horses up ahead. I knew better than to stop to say *hello*, but I fully intended to tip my hat as I rode past.

I never had a chance 'cause as we drew even with the settlers, a sharp *crack* sent Bear skittering sideways. The loud noise was followed by an ear-splitting *bang*. The settlers were shooting at me!

"Hey! Stop! Mail coming through!"
I screamed, looking frantically for a
place to hide. "Stop firing!"

My hand went to my pistol, but I
was already moving so fast that I figured I'd best not slow down, draw, and
aim.

As I flashed past the sorry-looking
group, I saw two men and a boy no
bigger than I was, reloading their guns!

"Lord Almighty, help me!" I hollered
to the high heavens. "Git up!" I hammered my heels against Bear's sides
and the poor horse, exhausted though
he was, plunged down the trail.

One last crack exploded behind us
and then we were too far past them —
unless they decided to come after us.
Hunched forward over the big horse's
withers I urged him on.

He tried, I know he tried, but Bear
stumbled hard and this time, I came
off.

I lay flat on my back on the trail
not able to move, not able to breathe.

After a moment, I lifted my head
and tried to suck in a little air.

"Whoa, Bear," I whispered. All I needed was for my horse to take off and those crazy settlers to come after me. But Bear wasn't going anywhere. His head hung low and his eyes were no longer soft and gentle. They were glazed with pain.

Joselyn, git on up. You're just winded. I rolled over onto my side, drew my knees up to my chest, and lay there in the dirt counting slowly to five. Every breath I drew hurt like the dickens. Now. Git up now. I pushed up onto my knees and stood.

Bear stayed where he was, blowing hard.

"Easy there, boy. What's wrong?"

Ignoring the ache in my own back I touched his neck and then moved slowly around to his other side. "Oh, Bear!" His haunch was split wide open. Blood oozed along the length of the wound and dribbled in dark red streaks down his hind leg.

We'd come around a bend and down a small hill so I couldn't see the wagons any more, but I knew the fools who'd shot my horse weren't far behind. I pulled my gun from its holster. Judging by how long we'd been riding, Cherry Bend had to be close by. With any luck, I wouldn't have to shoot anyone before I arrived.

I pulled at the mochila and slung it over my shoulders. Then I lifted off Bear's saddle and hid it behind some bushes at the side of the trail. Someone could come back for that later. Slipping the reins over the horse's head, I gave a gentle pull. Reluctantly, Bear followed me.

His head jerked with each painful step. Over and over we stopped. Over and over I made him walk on again.

I kept shifting the heavy mochila, but the stiff leather chafed against my neck. It was all I could do not to drop the danged thing and leave it for someone else to find.

With each step my back felt a bit better and I was able to breathe easier, but poor Bear was not so well off. It was harder and harder to get him going again after our little rests.

What a welcome sight it was when I finally spotted the peaked roof of the cabin at Cherry Bend. I let out a whoop loud enough to wake the dead and near dragged Bear off his feet trying to hurry him along.

Two men outside the cabin shouted back. When they saw I was on foot, they ran down the trail toward me, leading the fresh horse.

"Good Lord, son! What happened?"

"Would 'ya look at this?" the second man said from the other side of Bear. He held up his hand, fingertips crimson with fresh blood.

Bear's flanks heaved and white foam covered his neck.

"I got shot at," I said. "Is he hurt bad?"

The other man shook his head. "Don't look like it's too deep. We'll clean him up, stitch that wound, and give him some extra rest." He patted Bear's neck. "Come on, boy. You done good." The man took Bear from me. My heart tugged. I wanted to stay with the horse, make sure he was all right.

The first man, who I presumed to be the stationmaster, looked me up and down.

"Indians?" he asked.

"No, sir. Settlers."

"Settlers? For Pete's sake. What in tarnation do they think they're doing unloading buckshot into our good horses?"

"Don't rightly know," I said. My hands shook and I pressed them to my sides. "Their wagons are stuck in the mud back down the trail a mile or so. I reckon you could ride back and find out."

"Take my dog and my gun with me," he said grimly. Then he turned to me. "You all right to keep on going?"

I didn't feel right at all. My legs trembled and I felt queasy deep in my gut.

We both looked back in the direction of the settlers and then I nodded. Who knew when those crazy folk might just get it in their heads to come to the stationhouse looking to rob anyone they might find?

"Good. This here is Blackie." He helped me up onto the big, black thoroughbred whose white blaze gleamed as if someone had polished it up. The horse shifted uneasily and I patted his neck as much to calm myself as anything.

"Go, then," the stationmaster said. I turned Blackie and he knew just what to do.

"Godspeed!" the stationmaster shouted after me as we galloped away. I was beginning to understand just what the oath I had sworn really meant.

Mail first. Horse second. Rider last.

About half an hour past Cherry Bend, Blackie took a bad step and nearly went down.

Now what? I wondered, choking back tears.

"Whoa. Easy boy."

I tried to pull him up, but he kept trotting, limping badly.

"Whoa now," I insisted. The minute I was off his back, Blackie snaked his head out, and snatched a mouthful of grass.

"Sure. Think of your belly first."

He shifted his weight to ease the pressure on his left foreleg. "Easy, fella. Stand still. Let me have a look."

I squinted back along the trail, shielding my eyes against the sun's glare. An injury here meant a long walk back to Cherry Bend and, close as I could figure, just as far on to Butte. I chewed my bottom lip. Truth be told, if I didn't exactly feel happy riding fast along the trail, I felt real uneasy standing around just waiting for someone to come by and pick me off.

"Pa, what should I do?" Sure as day, Pa would not just stand around feeling sorry for himself. He'd look after his horse.

"How does that feel, boy?" I asked as I ran my hand down Blackie's leg. No heat or swelling — that was good.

"Pick it up." Without any trouble at all he let me check his foot. My, what a relief to see a sharp stone wedged between the soft frog and the back of his shoe. I fished out my penknife and worked at the stone, wiggling it back and forth until it popped out.

Blackie was happy enough after that and seemed sure of the way. As the day grew warmer, I almost managed to convince myself the ride was no more than a pleasant canter, the kind of easy gallop I used to take to condition young horses — except, of course, my backside ached from my fall. Every so often a shudder took hold of me as I thought of my horse getting shot out from underneath my saddle.

I watched for the fork in the trail just past the entrance to the box canyon Smokey McPhail had warned me about, but Blackie knew before I did to keep heading east.

We trotted on and on, cantering when the ground was level enough to allow it, walking when the way was steep or particularly rough. And each step of the way I agonized about how I was going to get out of my job.

Nearly three-and-a-half hours after leaving Ruby Valley, feeling like I'd been riding for eighty-two years, I cantered up to the house at Butte Station.

Three men waited with a fresh horse.

"Off you get. We've got Bill Winslow here ready to go. My name's Mr. Thomas."

Never in my life had I felt so happy to be sliding off the back of a horse.

"Steady now." I wasn't sure if the stationmaster was speaking to me or to Blackie, for my knees were so weak I could hardly stay upright.

"Fifty-nine seconds!" Mr. Thomas smacked the cantina shut and the sorrel mustang jumped forward, his rider holding onto his hat with one hand, the reins with the other.

"Y'er new," said a wiry little man with squinty eyes.

"Jo," I said, coughing to make my voice sound rougher.

"Hmph. They'll be sending us suckling babes before long."

"Arnie, I'll thank you to hold your tongue," Mr. Thomas said.

I flushed, glad of the coat of mud I wore on my face. Arnie couldn't have been much more than eighteen or nineteen himself.

"Joe, come in and have yourself some coffee," Mr. Thomas continued, extending his hand. "I suppose you might like some bacon and bread?"

I stuck my hand out to meet his, squeezing as tight as I could so he'd have no cause to think I was but a weakling girl.

"Yes, sir." At the thought of bacon, my mouth watered.

Arnie led Blackie away and I followed Mr. Thomas into the stationhouse. Inside, a young man with a mess of wild black hair hanging into his eyes sat on a three-legged stool by the fire.

"James — this is Joe. Joe — James."

James nodded in our direction. His tin mug rested on a table of rough planks. The cup of coffee Mr. Thomas poured from a battered tin coffeepot was near enough the best I'd ever tasted in my whole life.

"Have a good ride?" Mr. Thomas asked.

I shrugged and said, "Only got shot at once."

The two men stared at me. Apparently, being fired at didn't happen every day. That, I told myself, was a good thing to know.

"You hurt?" Mr. Thomas asked.

I shook my head.

"Lousy aim," wild-haired James said, slouching over his mug again.

"They got my horse," I said. "A gash on his flank is all. He'll be fine."

"Good to hear," Mr. Thomas said. "You can rest up here for a couple of days. We got patrols heading back toward Ruby Valley. They'll take care of any Indians fixing to ambush — "

"No sir," I interrupted. "Weren't no Indians. Was settlers with wagons that shot at me."

"Danged eastern folk shoot at anything that moves," James said, draining the rest of his coffee. "Next time anybody gives you trouble, put a bullet right here."

He jabbed his thumb into the spot right between his eyes. The way his crazy blue eyes glittered made me real nervous.

I looked away, over toward the bunks at the back. The dirt floor, I noticed, was soaking wet.

"Wet in here," I said.

Mr. Thomas grunted. "That there's the edge of the stream."

At first I thought he was pulling my leg, but the water moved slowly. It was seeping in under the cabin wall. The only area of the dirt floor that was well and truly dry was the narrow strip in front of the great stone hearth where we sat at the table.

With my belly full of bacon, biscuits, and beans, my eyelids drooped and Mr. Thomas pointed at an empty bunk. "Have a sleep," he said. There was no argument from me. I stepped over the muddy puddle and, though it was still early in the afternoon, crawled into an empty bunk.

But sleep didn't come easily. As I lay on the rough straw mattress, my arms and legs twitched and jerked as though I were still keeping my balance on a horse. My thoughts whirled and tumbled, each more unsettling than the next. Bear's blood-spattered leg, my fall on the trail, a thousand and one ways to get lost, shot, hurt, or killed on the trail made the twenty-five dollars a week seem like an insult.

Darn Will and Jackson anyway! I wondered where they were. Hauling nuggets of gold into the bank? Or lying dead at the bottom of some canyon?

Twenty-five dollars a week? It was still a lot of money, more than I could make doing laundry. How many weeks would I have to survive to earn what I needed? Ten more? Twelve?

I closed my eyes and tried to shut out the men's voices by remembering how Ma used to sing to me as I fell asleep, her gentle fingers lifting my hair from my forehead and letting it fall again. Still, my thoughts ran back and forth in my head as I lay there: tough it out and save enough to get set up in California or give up, confess I was a no-good liar, and go back to the orphanage in Carson City?

I rolled over to face the rough log wall and pulled my hat forward over my eyes. Well out of view, my face grew hot and soon my cheeks were wet with tears.

Eventually I dozed, but even then there was no rest. In my dreams, I galloped uphill and down, my horse scrambling over rocky trails and thundering across the wide, flat valley on the way into the next rest station. I thought I saw Ma and Pa standing beside Sarah on a hill. I whipped my horse to go faster, but then two wagons, driven by my brothers, picked up Sarah and my parents and carried them away. No matter how fast I went I couldn't catch them.

I slept fitfully until late afternoon when I sat bolt upright, my heart scrambling to climb right out of my chest.

Crack-crack-crack.

Gunfire!

Chapter Eight

I leapt out of bed and dropped to the floor, not caring that I was sprawled right in the mud.

My Lord, what was I gonna do now? Those crazy settlers had chased me here and right now as I hid inside, they were murdering Mr. Thomas, Arnie, James, and the other men!

Bang!

I jumped near out of my skin.

Bang! Bang!

Outside, men were shouting, but they didn't seem real worried. I recognized Arnie's voice.

"Your grandmother could shoot better than that!"

Several men laughed and a dog barked.

"Git out of my way, you dumb mongrel," James snarled.

"Come here boy," I heard Mr. Thomas call.

Bang! Bang!

More laughter followed the gunshots, and I slowly let out my breath. Shooting practice.

I sat at the table, my palms pressed flat against the rough grain of the planks until my hands stopped shaking. I had a few stern words to say to myself.

The fact of the matter was I was stuck. I thought of James's wild blue eyes and the red of his lips like a slash across his black, unkempt beard. The likes of him would not take kindly to finding out I was a girl.

Bang!

"Good shot, Thomas!"

What was the worst that could happen to me? I swallowed hard. If I ran into more trouble I might not live to see my thirteenth birthday. I closed my eyes and imagined I could feel Ma's hand gently stroking my hair. At least we would be together again — me, Ma and Pa, and the baby, Grace — if it came to that.

My hand moved to the pistol at my side. I might not want to be here, but there was no need to be foolhardy about things. If I was going to do this job right, I had to be ready to shoot and shoot well. Pushing open the stationhouse door, I stepped outside, blinking in the late afternoon sun.

"Well, lookee here," James said. It was all I could do not to turn tail and run.

Arnie, on one knee with his rifle to his shoulder, sighted down the barrel and took aim at a scarred stump about forty paces away.

James's stare never left my face. Just as Arnie pulled the trigger, James gave him a sharp poke in the side with the tip of his boot. The gun jumped back and Arnie leaped to his feet. "Who the — "

"Why, I bet even this young boy here could do better," James said, because of course the bullet had missed the mark by a mile. "Right, Joe?"

I took a deep breath. The last thing I wanted was to be the brunt of James's jokes.

"Go on, Joe. Give it a try," Mr. Thomas said kindly.

The stump hunkered there like a sullen dog, waiting for me to shoot. If I could just ignore James and the others, I might be all right. Pa had taught me to shoot. It would come back to me.

My pistol slid easily from its holster and I lifted it, feeling its weight in my hand. My arm straight, I leveled my hand and took aim. The tip of the pistol twitched ever so slightly from side to side and even as I pulled the trigger I knew I had missed the target.

"Shoots like a girl!" James crowed and I whirled around. "Just like you, Arnie!"

He was merely letting his cruel tongue wag, but I only just stopped myself from saying something stupid.

"Who's next?" Mr. Thomas asked. James swaggered forward. He fired off two quick shots, both of which hit the stump dead center.

"That's how it's done, boys," he said. "You keep on practicing and you might get the hang of it."

There was much groaning and cussing after he said that, and we kept shooting at the stump out back of the corral until it grew too dark to see. James didn't bother me any more than he bothered everyone else. Hard though it was, I said nothing in answer to his taunts and jeers. I just kept shooting and gave silent thanks to Pa for teaching me how to handle guns.

Though I wasn't exactly excited to go, when the time came two days after that, I headed out again, this time westbound. After that, I had quite a few good runs working the section of the mail route between Ruby and Butte Stations and on as far as Egan Canyon and Schell Creek. The farthest west I rode was to Robert's Creek, but only once when the westbound rider that was supposed to ride west from Ruby Valley fell ill from some bad meat.

I was starting to know the trail well. Each week for several weeks I added another twenty-five dollars to my California fund. But with the constant threat of ambush or being shot by confused settlers, the job didn't get any easier.

In fact, in the hottest part of the summer, things got a whole lot worse.

If I could have stopped my mind from wandering back to earlier times, I might have avoided the trouble I made for myself.

All too often I found myself thinking of Pa, the way he had with the stock, how his eyes lit up when Will first talked about California. Those memories were good, but others were sadder.

Ma and Baby Grace had died when I was but six. I didn't remember so much of Ma, but those things I could recall seemed as clear as if they'd happened only a few weeks before. "Joselyn," she'd say, pouring a large kettle of steaming water into a wash-tub, "Always remember: Cleanliness is next to Godliness."

When a terrible incident happened in the river not far from Jacob's Well, I was reminded of those baths that Ma insisted we take each week.

Cookie Townsend got it into his head he was in need of a bath. He stripped off his clothes and waded into the river. Trouble was Cookie Townsend plumb forgot he couldn't swim! Story goes he slipped when he bent over to wet his head. He didn't wash up onto shore until he'd drifted two miles downstream.

I suppose accidents like that were one reason why the men rarely bathed — once or twice a year when the weather was warm. They didn't find it strange I chose not to do so, either. But it never did feel right to me to be as filthy as a beast.

At least Cookie Townsend would have gone straight to the head of the line at the gates of Heaven. You couldn't get much Godlier than dying while you're having a bath. Then, I started fretting. What if something *did* happen to me on the trail and I got myself killed? I was so dirty Mrs. Pinweather could have shared a church pew with me without knowing who I was.

How unclean did you have to be before you couldn't get into Heaven at all? My fingernails were so black they looked like I'd been scratching at lumps of coal. The rest of me wasn't much better. I didn't have a change of clothes so those I wore day in and day out were filthy.

There I'd be after I died, talking to Saint Peter, explaining why I was so dirty. Ma and Baby Grace would be waving at me from inside Heaven. Ma's face would fall when she laid eyes on me.

So, I decided to have a bath – partly so I would be presentable if I died, and partly to celebrate my thirteenth birthday.

I found a pool in the creek downstream from the horse corral. The water wasn't overly deep — up to my knees where the creek went around a bend.

Checking that nobody was near, I slipped off my clothes. I gasped when the cold water swirled around my bare legs.

I bent over and scrubbed at my legs and feet with a sliver of black soap I'd put into my pocket earlier that day. My arms and face were next and then, already shivering, I held my breath and plunged my head under the water.

I scrubbed my fingers through my hair, but lasted only a few seconds before I had to stand straight up, coughing and sputtering and trembling with cold.

"Weeeell, lookee here."

Shrieking, I ducked under the water, trying to cover myself with my hands.

James stood on the bank, grinning down at me. "Joe? I'd say you was missing some parts."

My legs ached from squatting in the cold water and my heart hammered with terror. I couldn't run away — not without my clothes. Besides, where would I go? I couldn't fight him — James was too big, too strong. My tongue froze

in my head. All I could do was stare back at him.

"So maybe that's why you're so quiet all the time." His eyes raked over me and I hunkered down deeper into the water.

James took a step toward the edge of the creek. I inched backwards. Should I call out? Did it matter now if the whole camp knew? What would he do to me if I didn't shout for help?

"Shhhh," he said, almost like he knew what I was thinking. He crouched at the edge of the pool and raised his finger to his lips. "How about we make us a little deal, you and me."

Deal? I didn't care to make any kind of deal with wild-haired James. The water lapped and gurgled around me and my teeth chattered. I was hardly in a position to argue.

"Well, Miss Joe ... How about I don't say nothing about your little secret here and in return... "

He tugged at his beard as if considering the price of his silence. "In return, you can help me with a little job I got planned."

"What k-k-k-k-kind of — "

He touched his finger to his lips again. "I'll let you know in good time. Meantime, you'd best be getting on out of that crick or you'll catch your death of cold. We wouldn't want that, would we?"

For a long moment I thought he was going to stay where he was while I climbed out of the water. Then, without another word, he winked and walked away.

I crouched for as long as I could in case he came back. When he didn't, I counted to three and then burst from the pool, showering water behind me. I sprinted to my clothes and pulled them on, not caring in the least that I was still soaking wet. Tugging on my boots with shaking hands, I cursed under my breath. Darned fool James.

He was the last person in the world I would have trusted with my secret. Now what was I going to do? What was the job he had talked about? Feeling sick, I grabbed my hat and headed back to the stationhouse. Whatever he wanted me to do, it wasn't going to be good.

Chapter Nine

The weeks passed in a blur of mail runs through the heat of the desert summer. September brought shorter days and cool nights.

When I happened to be on a rest day at the same station as James, he treated me with exaggerated respect and called me Joe-boy. I longed for the days when James had tormented me for my poor shooting. Whenever I saw him, the knot in my stomach tightened as I waited for him to tell me what dreadful chore he had in mind.

Each week I counted my money, praying I would have enough to get away before James gave away my secret.

One night in late September, I was asleep in my bunk at Ruby Station dreaming of a great golden nugget, so big I couldn't lift it all by myself, when in my dream an earthquake started shaking the walls of my cabin.

"Joe-boy. I said, git up." A man grunted and I realized my bunk really was shaking. Hard.

"Joe-boy!" James's voice was loud and close to my ear.

I stiffened and choked back a scream.

"Shut-up and listen to what I got to say."

I licked my lips, my mouth bone dry.

James took a long, slow suck on a cigarette. Without warning, the bunk jerked again as he grabbed my collar and dragged me out of bed. His cigarette hung from between his lips and his hot breath stank something fierce as he leaned close and hissed at me,

"Here's what you're gonna do."

He pushed me against the wall, his knuckles pressed against my throat. "I overheard old Billy talking with the militia about a cash delivery headed for Sacramento this week."

He'd hardly started talking and I knew I didn't want to hear another word.

"A man like me could use some extra cash, don't you think?"

I squirmed and the hold on my shirt tightened.

"But it wouldn't be right for me, a Pony Express rider, to take off with a mochila full of cash now, would it?"

I managed the slightest shake of my head.

"'Course not. That's why you're gonna help me."

"Me?" My knees felt right peculiar, like my legs were made of dough.

"Who's due to head west tomorrow afternoon?" he asked.

"Me," I whispered.

"That's right. And this is what's gonna happen. You ride west just like always except you're gonna make an unscheduled stop at them smelly pools just past Diamond Springs. You know the ones I mean?"

I nodded. I knew exactly where he meant. The ponds smelled of bad eggs. No man or beast would stop there without darned good reason. The stationhouse not far from there was known as Sulphur Springs.

"Wait for me there. I'll bring a second mochila stuffed with paper." James chuckled and I stared at the glowing tip of his cigarette as it hopped up and down in the dark.

"We'll switch mochilas and you'll ride on to Dry Creek with the worthless one and deliver it just like nothing happened. I'll be back here at Ruby before anyone knows there's a problem."

He twisted my shirt tighter. I whimpered and tried to push his hand away.

"Shut-up," he said. "You do as I say or — "

By the dim glow of his cigarette his forefinger aimed at my temple.

"You got that?"

I nodded again, my knees buckling out from under me.

"Now git back into bed and keep yer mouth shut."

I scrambled back into my bunk. Not long after that the door to the stationhouse creaked open. Uncle Billy slid the bolt home and poked at the embers of the fire. He and his dog had been out checking the livestock.

"Time to rest your old bones, dog." Springs creaked as the dog jumped onto an empty bunk. "Evening, James."

"Evening, sir."

The two men fell to chatting quietly.

I could not sleep for anything, not even after the men were breathing deep and regular. A cash delivery. Bolivar Roberts had talked about them what seemed like a hundred years ago in Carson City.

James was going to rob the mail and I was going to be most important to him if his plan was going to work. James would tell my secret in a second if I breathed a word of what I'd been told to anyone — if he didn't shoot me first.

I was beside myself. James had worked things so it looked like I was part of the robbery. The only way to explain why I was going along with it was to explain how he had found out I was really a girl. If the Express Company knew I'd lied about that, then why would they believe I was innocent of the robbery? I was so close to being able to go to California I couldn't bear the thought of having to give up now. For the first time in a long time, I cried myself to sleep.

It seemed but five minutes later and I was up again. For most of the day James never let me out of his sight. Before I knew what had happened, we were outside the stationhouse waiting for the westbound rider.

"Maybe you won't have too much snow." James squinted at the gray clouds hanging low over the hills looking for all the world like he was truly interested in the weather. James didn't always help with the horses. I knew he was there to stop me from saying anything to Uncle Billy.

"Whoa, Jess." I patted the chestnut mare, the horse that would carry me west. She'd been saddled for an hour and now pricked her ears toward the end of the valley.

"What do you see there, girl?" I asked.

The mare whinnied, her belly tucked up and quivering. A horse and rider, at first just a moving dot, grew larger as they galloped toward us.

A minute later Bart Ridley jumped off a black mustang and gave me a slap on the back.

"Good to see you, Joe. Make good speed, you hear? Smells like snow out there." He winked and grinned at me, unaware of my near panic.

James slipped the mochila over the saddle and slapped his gloved hand against the saddle. Jess danced on the spot and it took two of us to hold her.

"Up you get, Joe," James said, as Uncle Billy pulled the time card from the unlocked pouch. I climbed up into the saddle, Billy noted the time, slipped the card back into the pouch, and sent us off with a wave of his hat.

The mare spun in a circle and we were gone.

We settled into a quick canter and I glanced down at the three locked pouches of the mochila.

James would soon set out to follow me. It would be easy enough for him to leave. The men often headed out to hunt. It was such a simple plan — switch mochilas, take the money, and send the empty saddlebags on to California. He must have borrowed one of the spares kept at the bigger stations in case of damage or theft. I supposed he planned to replace it as soon as he'd made the switch and taken the money.

By the time anyone discovered that the money was missing, the borrowed mochila would be back in place, James would have long disappeared, and nobody would be any the wiser. As Jess charged up a short ridge, I wondered how much cash was in the bags.

As we topped the rise, I saw fires burning in the hills ahead. Indians, most likely. For the thousandth time I thought of Sarah and her people and hoped she had escaped the recent battles alive.

Pulling my hat down over my ears, I put my spurs to the mare's sides. Jess jumped forward. In places snow lay upon the trail, but not deeply, so I made good time to horse changes in Jacob's Well and Diamond Springs.

The sun dropped as I left the stationhouse at Diamond Springs and headed up the trail toward James at the sulphur ponds. How long would I have to wait before James would catch up to me?

The impending robbery loomed. What if I were caught with the empty mochila? I'd go to jail where my secret would be discovered. Even if I were found innocent of any part in the robbery, my career as an Express rider would be over. Then I had another thought to add to my worries. What if James was planning to shoot me so I couldn't ever tell what I knew? That would make the whole thing seem like a good old-

fashioned hold-up. Shoot the rider —
take the money.

My new horse, Runaway Luke, galloped into the gathering darkness. The
first time I'd ridden at night I had been
terrified of losing my way. I soon learned
that the night is rarely completely black
— the stars and moon usually provided
enough light that we hardly had to slow
down at all. I remembered how Smokey
McPhail had told me that I would be
grateful to my horse for having such
good eyes in the dark. Smokey had sure
been right. The horses were far more
comfortable in the dark than I was and
kept a quick pace in all but the blackest
of nights.

Despite my thudding heart, I reached
along Luke's neck and gave him an
encouraging pat. There was so little
time. I had a job to do — get the mail
through — but how?

I reached for the pistol tucked into
my holster. Over the past weeks I'd
become more than a fair shot, though
I'd never had to shoot at anything bigger
than a jackrabbit.

But shooting James at the sulphur pools was too risky. He'd likely have his gun drawn, just in case I tried something like that. He'd be quick enough to put a bullet through my head. *Bang!* That would be me, gone. If I shot him first then I'd be a murderer, not just an accomplice to a robbery.

Back and forth the arguments went in my mind. If I didn't shoot him, he'd get away with the money. I would have helped, and for that I could land in jail or maybe even be hanged! If I did try to shoot him, I'd likely wind up dead myself.

The mail came first, that was true, but was I really supposed to get myself shot in order to make the delivery? And how, if I got myself shot, was I supposed to save the mail anyway?

There seemed no answer. "Whoa, Luke," I said, pulling him back to a trot. No need to hurry.

What if I didn't ride to the station at Sulphur Springs at all? What about turning around and going back to Diamond Springs? I could explain everything to the stationmaster. But James, with his nasty scowl and skill with a pistol, was somewhere behind me.

I looked back over my shoulder. Every shadow loomed huge and threatening. I shuddered and urged Runaway Luke into a faster trot.

We rode into a valley as the moon was rising, bright enough to throw shadows across the trail. We loped along easily, the footing good and Luke still strong and willing beneath me. I glanced south across the valley and noticed a break in the hills. And that was when the idea came to me. Maybe I could ride around the station at Sulphur Springs, bypass the horse change there, and head straight for the next station. That would be Robert's Creek.

It was the best idea I'd had so far. If nothing else, the extra miles would give me more time to think.

I turned Luke from the trail and headed across the valley toward the small canyon. I'd ridden Luke before. He was a good horse, strong and eager. If any animal could make the extra distance, it was the big roan. We wound our way back up into the mountains working our way westward in what I hoped was a direction more or less parallel to the main trail.

Chapter Ten

Hours later, halfway up the side of a deep gully, Luke stumbled. The roan was tired. His head hung low when I hopped off to lead him the rest of the way to the top. Not far from where we crested the ridge, a stream trickled through the rocks. I led him to drink and he followed close behind me like a big dog.

The moon was high and we'd had little trouble picking our way along Indian trails.

"Have a good drink, boy."

I kneeled to drink from the icy water

but the empty ache in my belly hardly faded. How long had I been in the saddle? We'd climbed in and out of valleys, at first heading southwest and then trying to make our way northwest again so we'd rejoin the trail well past Sulphur Springs. I didn't think it would be long before we were back on the main wagon trail.

Every so often we saw Indian fires flickering high on the sides of the hills. I steered well clear of these, not wanting any more trouble on my hands. Back in the saddle, I rode on and on, across another wide valley and up into the hills beyond. Still there was no sign of the deep wagon ruts.

I didn't think I had crossed the trail by mistake. There had been plenty of traffic over the summer and not that much snow yet, even at the highest points. I pulled Luke up again near another stream and tried to get my bearings in the dark. We should have met the trail again by now, but all I saw around us were endless mountains and valleys. We were well and truly lost. I swallowed hard.

Luke snatched hungrily at whatever thin blades of grass he could find. The moon tucked in behind a cloud and the darkness deepened. Luke's crunching sounded louder than ever and then, suddenly, it stopped. Luke yanked his head up and pricked his ears forward. I strained to see through the dark and fumbled for my gun as two figures emerged from the darkness. Indians.

"Who's there?" I asked.

A hand reached out and caught Luke's bridle.

"Hey!" The cry strangled in my throat. I raised my hand to shoot but in the moment I hesitated, not knowing which of the two men to shoot first, the second man grabbed my wrist and wrenched my gun away.

The first man turned Luke and began to lead him toward one of the fires I'd seen on the hills.

My mind, exhausted, was blank. I was no match for the two men, especially without my pistol. Even in my dreadful state, I knew there was a good chance the men were Paiutes.

"Wait! Do you know Sarah Winnemucca?" I asked, desperate to save myself.

The man who was leading Luke nodded brusquely but didn't stop. "What about Chief Winnemucca? Or Natchez? Chief Numaga?" I tried to remember other names Sarah had mentioned.

The two Indians stopped and spoke in their language. Then they turned away from the fire on the hill and headed in the opposite direction.

"Where are you going? I don't mean you any trouble. I've got to take the mail to — "

It was hopeless. Even if they understood me, why should they believe me? I was nowhere near the trail.

Soon we came to several stick huts shaped like squat beehives.

"Down."

I slid from Luke's back and stood, shivering. Even though it was the middle of the night, people were moving around, most of them going in and out of a slightly larger hut a little away from the others. Someone sang and several others chanted.

One of the men who had led me to the camp called out and a young woman emerged from the bigger hut and came toward us.

"Sarah!"

I took a step forward, ready to embrace her, but she stepped back and stared at me, her arms folded over her chest.

"Who are you?"

"It's me! Joselyn!" I pulled off my hat. Sarah stared at me for a moment. Then she chuckled.

"Your hair!" she said and reached over to touch my shorn locks.

The two men spoke and pointed back in the direction we'd come from.

"They thought you were a scout," Sarah said.

"Why didn't they kill me?"

"You would have more information if you were alive. Why are you here?"

I explained and Sarah shook her head. "This is a hard path you have chosen to get to California."

I had to laugh at that.

"I am pleased our men found you. The wagon trail is like this — " She made a slashing motion with her hand side to side through the air. "And you are going like this — " The second line she made was just below and parallel to the first. The way I'd been travelling I might never have crossed the trail.

"He will show you," she said, nodding toward one of the men who had found me. "I cannot come. My grandfather, Truckee, is very sick. We, the old, the women and children, and a few men have been hiding here, away from the fighting at Pyramid Lake. But Grandfather is very ill. We have lit fires in the hills to call our people in so they might — " Her voice cracked. " — so they might say goodbye."

"Sarah — "

"Shh. Say nothing. There is nothing to say. But I must stay with him."

I nodded. How well I understood. Ma, Pa, and even Baby Grace, whom I had known such a short time, had not passed over to God's care alone.

Sarah glanced back over her shoulder at the hut where her grandfather lay dying, her eyes brimming with tears. She turned back to me and took my hands in hers.

"You know what you must say about seeing us here."

I nodded. "Nothing."

"And when my people are friends once again with yours, I never met a girl called Joselyn on a Pony Express horse."

We both smiled. "I'd like to go back to California one day. Maybe I will see you there."

"I'd like that," I said and squeezed her hands.

She nodded, then pulled away and returned to her grandfather.

I mounted my horse once again. The man who was to be my guide said nothing but nudged my knee with something solid. My pistol.

"Thank you," I said as I took it from him.

He indicated I should follow him and then led me some distance before saying, "Go past there." He pointed at a single scraggly pine tree in the distance, a black shape against the night sky.

I thanked him again. He patted Luke on the rump and disappeared into the darkness.

Never in my life had I felt so alone.

Chapter Eleven

"Come on, Luke. If he says to go past the tree, we go past the tree. We'll find the trail and the station. What a good feed you'll have ... What a bed there will be for me!"

Sounding cheerful was a strain, but I needed to keep my spirits up as we set off, uphill, toward the big tree.

When we finally stood atop the ridge, we were both blowing and panting. I opened my jacket to the chill pre-dawn air. Back toward the east, the undersides of the gray clouds were tinged with pink and yellow. As I watched, the colors warmed until the clouds were a deep blush of rose.

Turning my back on the rising sun and the scraggly pine, I urged Luke into a plodding trot.

The morning was the strangest I had ever seen. Even as the sun rose higher in the sky, the clouds thickened and built so the day hardly grew brighter. Within an hour a bitter, freezing rain was falling. I pulled my collar up around my neck, my hat down over my ears and hunched into the saddle. Soon the relentless pelt of raindrops had mixed with snow and soaked us both.

Though I wore thick calfskin gloves, my fingers grew numb. I had to tuck first one hand and then the other inside my jacket to keep them from freezing. I imagined James arriving at the stinky ponds and wondered what he'd do when he saw I wasn't there.

The mud froze into treacherous ruts and bumps. These became more and more difficult to see as the snow thickened and blanketed everything. We pressed on, eyes slits against the driving snow. Once Luke stopped and looked back at me, his long eyelashes white with frost. Every step became a torment as Luke slipped and slid. We had long passed the tree and still there was no sign of the wagon trail. Could the Indian have lied?

I willed Luke to keep going. And he did until, without warning, he stumbled.

"Come on, boy," I pleaded, putting my heels to the exhausted horse's sides. "Git up!"

But Luke refused to budge. The poor animal turned his tail to the wind and would not take another step.

I climbed out of the saddle and moved to Luke's head. Just as I reached for his bridle I, too, stumbled. The trail! That's why Luke had tripped. We had found the wagon ruts, invisible beneath the freshly fallen snow.

"Hallelujah!" I shouted and slapped the horse on the neck. "Thank you!" I shouted into the swirling snow. It was agony to haul myself back onto Luke's back

Buffeted from behind by blasts of wind, I turned Luke westward. Only then did the big horse agree to walk on.

It was impossible to say exactly where we were, but I figured we couldn't be too far from Robert's Creek. For a short while my heart skipped and sang with the joy of knowing we would soon be safe.

Hah! Had I learned nothing? The snow began in earnest. Burning pinpricks whipped across my cheek, searing my face. Soon I was so cold I could barely stay upright in the saddle. We had to move faster or we would never make it to shelter.

"Come on, Luke my friend, let's git on home."

Luke dropped his head and reluctantly picked up a jog.

Snow whirled around us as the wind shifted directions — first blasting us from the side, then attacking from the front. My nose, cheeks, hands, legs, and even my mind were numb. With fingers thickened by cold, I fumbled to tie my kerchief across my face. Before I had it in place, it was soaked through. I tried to wiggle my toes inside my boots but could scarcely feel them at all. How I longed to stomp around in front of a roasting fire, a steaming mug of Arbuckle's cradled in my hands.

Some time after we'd joined the trail Luke tripped again, this time over a tree root. He slithered on the icy ground as he struggled to keep his feet under him. It was hard to say how far we'd come. But we had ridden through the night, so old Luke had been working hard for twelve hours straight and I'd been in the saddle for longer than that.

When the horse slipped again in the wet snow, the time had come for me to dismount and travel along on foot.

"Holy crow!" I shouted, hopping from one foot to the other. Sharp pains shot up my legs. My feet felt huge — ten times their regular size. I had to look down to see that they had not split my boots wide open. I hobbled along, my feet protesting with every step as we slogged through the snow.

"Mail first. Horse second. Me last," I chanted in time to Luke's muffled hoof beats. Crazy laughter bubbled and churned inside me. I imagined myself warm and cozy as I lay down in the soft snow, drifting off to sleep.

"Mail first ... horse second ... "

Once I fell and grabbed for Luke's mane. He paid no heed but plugged along, his eyes half-closed against the relentless wind.

More and more often he stumbled and then, at the top of an embankment, he stopped altogether.

"Git on up!" I yelled as fiercely as I could, and smacked him across the haunches.

I cried, then, the first and only time of the whole journey, for it broke my heart to hit an animal who had given his all for me under the most miserable conditions.

But what else could I do? Leave him there to freeze or be devoured by the wolves I'd heard howling not so far away? Wolves aren't so stupid as to take on an armed rider and a healthy horse, but an exhausted animal left to his own devices was another matter.

Weeping, I reached back and gave him another smack with a switch. He skidded down the bank to the creek at the bottom, crashing to his knees.

"Easy, boy. Easy."

I pressed my cheek against his neck and rubbed him between the ears.

"Come on. You can get up." I tugged at his bridle and Luke heaved himself to his feet. We splashed through the stream and I cried out as the ice-cold water seared my frozen feet. I staggered away from the creek, sick with the knowledge that neither Luke nor I could travel much farther.

I thought of my beautiful ma and the sister I never knew. I spoke a word to my dead pa and cursed my brothers who had left me in Carson City. I offered up prayers for me, for Sarah and her grandfather, and for Luke, and then I nearly jumped out of my skin because right behind me Luke let out a loud whinny.

Coming back through the snow was the most welcome sound ever — an answering whinny.

Chapter Twelve

I couldn't have cared less whether the other horse belonged to a crazy gun-toting settler or even to James himself. I shouted as loud as I could and made my way toward the answering calls.

When, a few minutes later, the stationhouse emerged from the swirling snowstorm, I near enough fainted away with relief.

"Joe? Where in tarnation are you comin' from?" the stationmaster asked, inspecting the time card before signing it and slipping it back into the pouch.

With much rushing around and shouting, two men readied a new horse in record time. A rider I didn't know mounted up to continue the ride west.

"This ain't Robert's Creek," I finally had a chance to say.

The stationmaster laughed and shook his head.

"Robert's Creek is about thirty miles behind you. This here is Dry Creek."

I opened my mouth and shut it again. How far had I traveled? Ninety miles? A hundred? More?

Far enough, I'd say.

"Come on in out of the cold and tell me what happened. You can tell Simpson and Wood from the militia, too. They arrived not long ago looking for you when you didn't show up at Sulphur Springs or Robert's Creek. We figured you'd been robbed. Shot dead."

The four men huddled by the fire in the unfinished stationhouse and looked expectantly at me. As I told them my story, gusts of wind lifted the canvas tarp they had tied over the space where the roof should have been.

"We gotta get ourselves a roof before we get any *bad* weather," one of the men joked.

I grinned despite the pain in my feet as they started to thaw. They hurt even more than when they were frozen, if such a thing were possible.

I told the men how James had planned to rob the mail. "James said he'd kill me if I got in the way."

The stationmaster nodded. "You done the right thing, coming here," he said.

The two men from the army pulled on their coats.

"We'll head back toward Sulphur Springs, see if we can find James."

"Wait," I said, reaching for my boots. "I'm coming."

"You ain't going nowhere," the stationmaster said.

Part of me wanted to say, "Fine — I'll stay right here by the fire." But another part of me, an angry part I never knew I had, was itching to see James hauled away to jail. I knew exactly where the drop-off was. I could show the soldiers. Maybe James had left the second mochila there. Maybe he was still waiting at the sulphur pools.

"Try to stop me," I said, my hand moving over my pistol.

"Whoa now, boy!"

But we didn't have a chance to finish the argument because, right then we heard scuffling outside and the door burst open sending a cloud of wet snowflakes scurrying across the floor.

A man's bulky frame filled the doorway. Snow clung to his beard and he stamped the snow from his boots. It was James.

"I'm looking for a certain Joe Whyte — a lowdown thief I believe is headed this — "

Then he saw me.

Without stopping to think I leapt to my feet and pulled out my pistol, aiming it at the point right between his eyes.

"That's him!" I said. "That's James!"

This was not the welcome James had expected. His wild blue eyes widened as he stared at me and my gun. Then he turned tail and ran out into the snow, the two militiamen and the stationmaster hot on his heels.

He didn't get but three feet before they brought him to the ground, dragged him back inside and arrested him.

The men tied James hand and foot to a bunk. We took turns watching over him. When it was my turn, I kept my pistol close at hand. Every so often James scowled at me and spat on the floor.

He looked awful scrawny all tied up like that and I wasn't afraid of him no more.

"So how come you were reporting your own robbery?" I asked when the others were outside tending the stock and splitting more firewood.

He glowered at me, but after a time he answered. "Figgered you tried to take my money. If I weren't going to get it back, at least I could get a reward," he said.

Reward? I hadn't thought of a reward.

I don't know what got into me then. I suppose I felt brave seeing as how I had my pistol and James was trussed

up like a Christmas goose. But I asked him right out, "So, you gonna tell?"

He sneered at me and laughed a short, nasty bark of a laugh.

"What? And tell them a *girl* stopped me from getting what I wanted?" He shook his head. "I been in jail before and I've got out before. I'll git out again. And when I do, *Miss* Joe, don't you think I won't be coming to find you."

I swallowed hard but kept my chin up and met his gaze with my own. "You can look," I said. "But you ain't going to find me. And if you do, don't think I wouldn't use this." I raised my pistol and he shifted uneasily.

I could have put a bullet between that snake's eyes right then and there. But I didn't. It wouldn't have been right.

When the snow stopped, the militiamen rode up to Sulphur Springs where they found the mochila stuffed with paper. That, and my statement, was all the evidence they needed to take James to the jailhouse in Carson City. The next day I headed back up to Ruby Valley.

All the regulars were there but so was Bolivar Roberts. He slapped me on the back and said, "You're one of the best, Joe. And, the Company looks after its best."

"Thank you, sir. Mail first. Pony second. Rider last."

He winked and said, "That may be so. But a pony can't use a reward. I suspect you can." I sure didn't know what to say when Mr. Roberts gave me a cash reward for saving the mail. I don't suppose it was even close to whatever was in the mailbags, but when I added the money to what I'd saved of my wages I had more than enough for my coach ticket to California. Not only that, I had enough to keep myself through the winter and buy a mule and enough equipment so I'd be able to head to the gold fields just as soon as the weather was warm enough in the spring.

I'd miss running the mail. But near as anybody could tell, they wouldn't need riders much longer. The telegraph was coming along fast as anything. As soon as the lines from east and west joined up, there wouldn't be any more call for a mail service like the Pony Express.

I didn't know whether I was going to find my brothers, but as each day went by I cared a little less whether I ever saw them again. If we ever did meet up, my, wouldn't I just give those boys a piece of my mind! And if not, well, it seemed to me there was enough gold out that way for anyone who dared to look and who wasn't afraid of a little hard work. Maybe Sarah would make another trip to California and we could be friends again.

I ran my fingers along the outside of my leather holster. Panning for gold couldn't be more dangerous than riding back and forth through Utah Territory, could it?

I, for one, couldn't wait to find out.

Author's Note

Jo's Triumph was inspired by the stories of several remarkable women of the west: Charlotte Parkhurst, who cut off her hair, dressed as a boy, and became known as one of the finest stagecoach drivers of the 1850's and 60's; Sarah Winnemucca, an advocate and spokeswoman for the Paiute Indians who lived for a time at Ormsby House and witnessed the incident with the Washo Indians; and Sarah Emma Edmonds, who disguised herself as a man and joined the Union Army as Franklin Thompson.

The Pony Express operated between April, 1860, and November, 1861. A section of the trail not far from Carson City was closed temporarily when hostilities between the Paiutes and the settlers were at their worst. Though the general context of *Jo's Triumph* is rooted in fact, I have taken liberties with specific dates and locations, invented a couple of Pony Express stations, and pressed others into service slightly ahead of time in order to accommodate Jo's fictional adventure. Where historical sources differed, I chose to use those accounts which best suited the requirements of this novel.

Though numerous orphanages were in existence at the time, the Carson City Home for Unfortunate Girls and all its inhabitants are figments of my imagination.

Major Ormsby, the Williams brothers, Chief Numaga, Uncle Billy, Bolivar Roberts, and several others mentioned in the text are all historical figures who might well have met Joselyn Whyte had she been alive at the time this story takes place.

If you are interested in reading more about this time in history, the following titles provide information about the Pony Express, the Pyramid Lake War, and the life of Sarah Winnemucca:

Life Among the Piutes (sic): Their Wrongs and Claims
Sarah Winnemucca Hopkins
Chalfont Press, 1969

The Pony Express
Peter Anderson
The Children's Press (Grolier), 1996

The Pony Express in Nevada
Dorothy Mason for the Nevada Bureau of Land Management
Nevada State Museum, 1996

Sand in A Whirlwind: The Paiute Indian War of 1860
Ferol Egan
Doubleday & Company, Inc., 1972